FRA[illegible]

UNICORN

ALPACA

Gavin Puckett

Illustrated by India Joseph

faber

FOR RILEY AND RUBY – GP
FOR SUNNY – IJ

First published in 2024
by Faber & Faber Limited
The Bindery,
51 Hatton Garden,
London EC1N 8HN
faber.co.uk

Typeset in Minion by Faber
Printed by CPI Group (UK) Ltd, Croydon CR0 4YY

A CIP record for this book is available from the British Library

ISBN 978–0–571–36962–1

Printed and bound in the UK on FSC® certified paper in line with our continuing commitment to ethical business practices, sustainability and the environment.
For further information see faber.co.uk/environmental-policy

2 4 6 8 10 9 7 5 3 1

ABOUT THE AUTHOR

GAVIN PUCKETT is an award-winning children's author from South Wales, where he lives with his wife, son and their beloved cat, George. He wrote the hilarious Fables from the Stables series as well as *Blanksy the Street Cat*. His favourite word is bibliobibuli and he was once bitten by a squirrel when he was twelve.

ABOUT THE ILLUSTRATOR

INDIA JOSEPH is an illustrator and talking therapist from Manchester. She was Highly Commended in the FAB Prize. She enjoys documentaries, stories about ghosts and loves pigs so much she has one tattooed on her leg.

Now here's a tall tale (in fact it's a cracker)

All about Frank, a curious alpaca.

By that, I mean different,

strange in his ways,

Bringing untold commotion

to each of his days.

Although Frank's daily life appeared

simple enough,

Frank was SOOOO NERVOUS,

it made things quite tough!

You see . . .

Frank lived in a zoo,
  a place where you'd find
Lots of cuddly creatures –
  the soft, petting kind.

Of course, there were other things
  found in this zoo,
Such as tigers, gorillas and elephants too.

ZOO
WELCO

DO NOT
TOUCH!

But these were locked up

in enclosures or cages,

In case they had moments

of fury or rages.

They were rather unruly

(not nasty as such).

Just their temperament meant . . .

you could look but not touch!

Frank's section was huggable,

lovely and warm.

A place where the parents and children

would swarm.

Folk here could cuddle and

nuzzle the features

Of any adorable small, fluffy creatures.

There were bunnies and micropigs,

sheep with white fleeces.

Pygmy goats, wallabies, ducklings

and geeses . . .

Guinea pigs, hamsters with

soft, fuzzy hair.

If you're looking for cuteness,

you'd find it right there!

Bryan the hamster was ever so sweet,

With his cute squidgy nose

and his little pink feet.

Molly the goat had a coat

that shone bright.

Whereas Elsie the pig's was quite

bristly and tight.

The kiddies could feed them
and play with them too
(Being terribly careful to
not step in poo!).

And . . .

The animals here were

permitted to roam,

Every inch of the building they

each called their home.

It was life as it should be!

Delightfully fun.

Every animal loved it . . .

Well, all except one.

That's right, it was Frank.

This alpaca was tense!

Awfully stressed in the jittery sense.

He was wary of children

who came to the place . . .

And the way that they squeezed

and they squashed his cute face.

SQUISH

He would shriek if, by chance, a child
wandered near,
Before scarpering off in complete
fits of fear.

Frank didn't like crowds –

he hated the fuss,

And his whole body zinged with

complete anxiousness.

It was probably down to one simple fact –

A ridiculous reason to be quite exact . . .

Frank thought he looked silly!

For reasons unknown.

So he chose to spend every day

on his own.

In Frank's mind, his daft ears
and tight, curly hair –
Well surely that made him
the silliest there.

Combined with his neck (which was
slender and long),
It would make people laugh . . .
and that was just wrong!

It meant Frank missed out
on the love and exposure
Enjoyed by the rest in his
gorgeous enclosure.

Elsie tried to involve him,
but Frank would say no,
And would hardly dare put
his fine features on show.

Bryan tried too – as did
most of the others
Like Molly and each of her
sisters and brothers.

But despite their best efforts,
Frank wouldn't give in,
As he just wasn't comfortable
in his own skin.

If only he saw what his
friends could all see.
The kindness, the cuteness,
his fine pedigree.

Then . . . instead of the sadness,
perhaps he'd feel pride,
Or a sense of belonging,
with no need to hide.

One warm summer's evening,

at twenty past eight,

As the customers all left in droves

through the gate . . .

Frank crept from the corner,
relieved by the sight
That the children had all scuttled
off for the night.

'At last, they've all gone!' he said with a smile
(A quiet enclosure was far more his style).

He sat by the door and looked out
at the grounds
'Mid the calmness and typical animal
sounds.

The stalls were secured, with their
shutters all drawn,
And the fairground attractions had
closed until morn.

ROAR!

CHEEP

CHEEP!

SCREEEEECH!

The Ferris wheel glistened
beneath twinkling stars,
And the zookeepers each made
their way to their cars.

The petting enclosure was quieter too,
With the creatures discussing the day
they'd been through.

Bryan was exhausted from

all the commotion,

The constant attention and children's devotion.

The goats were so fuzzy from

petting that some . . .

Looked like electricity had surged

through their bum!

Elsie seemed pleased and –

although she was spent –

She felt nothing but happy,

relaxed and content.

But not poor Frank, he still
felt quite tense,
And his tummy did somersaults
filled with suspense.

'Time for my bed,' uttered Frank,
feeling hollow,
Knowing the same things would
happen tomorrow.

But . . .

As Frank passed the micropigs

snug in their sty . . .

A rather peculiar thing caught his eye.

In the distance, a book had been
dropped by a child,
And its cover was dazzling,
vivid and wild.

On the front was an animal
(that much Frank knew),
But he'd never seen this kind before
in a zoo.

The body was white, mixed
with glittery sprinkles,
Which shimmered and
glimmered with fairy-like
twinkles.

Its tail was bright pink, like
the mane on its head.
'My goodness, what's this?'
a curious Frank said.

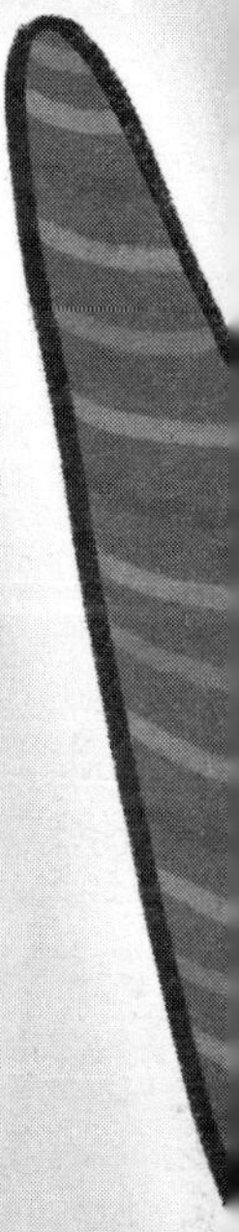

That's when he saw it – a large golden horn –
And a title above it that read . . .

UNICORN.

'A UNICORN, wow!' exclaimed Frank
in surprise,
Amazed by the beauty in front of his eyes.

He flicked through the pages and
glanced at the features
That told of these magical,
mythical creatures.

The pictures were great, and
the paragraphs packed,
With every known fabulous UNICORN fact.

Like how they were brave,

oh so trendy and slick,

Delightfully playful and

fiendishly quick . . .

Stylish and handsome and

ever so topical.

Found only in places exotic and tropical.

Frank got lost in that book,

read it cover to cover.

It was cleverly written – unlike any other.

So he picked up his find from

the dusty old floor,

Took it back to his pen and

he read it some more!

'Incredible, wonderful, st-st-stunning,'

he stuttered.

'I wish *I* was a UNICORN, really!' he uttered.

Frank wetted his hoof before

twisting the curls

On his head to a point

made from long, hairy swirls.

Then he pouted his lips, and

he checked his reflection.

Two words came to mind . . .

sheer perfection!

‘If only I wasn’t this silly alpaca,

A loser, a failure, a panicky slacker.

‘Give me some glitz and

a horn on my head . . .

‘Then folks wouldn’t laugh –

they’d all love me instead!’

The next morning came

(like it usually does)

And soon the enclosure was

packed with a buzz.

THE GREAT BIG BOOK OF
unicorns

Frank scampered off to a corner less loud,
Like he normally did to escape from
the crowd.

Once he was safe, he collapsed in a heap,
Closed both his eyes, and then fell
off to sleep.

Clutching his book, Frank soon
started dreaming,
Of 'a UNICORN'S life' – an existence
with meaning.

Of days filled with happiness,
stardom and fame,
Where children and parents would
chant out his name.

And that's when it happened!
Something so great . . .
A magical, fairy-tale twist of pure fate.

Out in the yard, by the food and drink stand,
Young Tim clutched an ice-cream cone
tight in his hand.

ICE CREAM
COLD DRINKS

Tim's mum had bought three . . .

One for her, one for Tim . . .

And another for Tim's older sister

named Kim.

While up in the rafters a seagull

Called Phil patiently waited,

all quiet and still.

Phil's eyes opened wide

and lit up with delight,

As he leaped from the beam,

spread his wings and took flight . . .

Then just as young Tim poked

his tongue out to lick

That glistening gelato,

all creamy and thick . . .

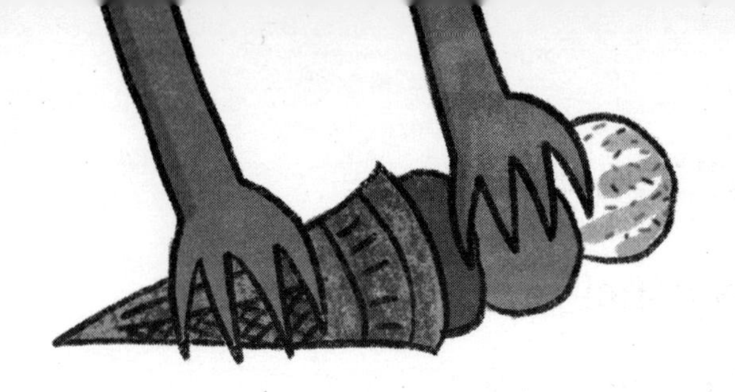

Phil muscled in with a squawk
and a shriek . . .
And snatched up the poor boy's cone
in his beak!

Young Tim cried out, 'NOOOOOO!'
all sad and distraught
(It seemed he'd not gripped it as tight
as he'd thought!).

'Come back!' Tim yelled out.

'That's my cone!' was his cry,

As sneaky Phil flapped and

continued to fly . . .

Holding his loot (and of course –

his composure)

Over the zone of the petting enclosure.

But . . .

Phil didn't get far

(at least so I am told),

As he realised that ice cream is

terribly cold.

He let go of the cone and it fell

from the sky . . .

Before landing on top of

Frank's head nearby!

Frank bolted up with a look of surprise
And he caught his reflection through
  sleep-ridden eyes.

'What's this . . . ?' he enquired with
  a quizzical face,
Feeling the heart in his chest
  start to race.

He glanced at his body and cried,
  'Goodness me!
'I'm covered in sprinkles.
  How could this be?

'Wait . . .

There's a horn on my head . . .

ALL MY DREAMS

HAVE COME TRUE!

'I'M A UNICORN!

YIPPEE-YAY,

WHOOPIE-DOO!'

At that very moment, something
went click.
A complete transformation that
happened so quick.

For once in his lifetime, Frank
wasn't scared;
He was oozing with confidence,
bold and prepared.

He pranced from his shack, looking
rather outrageous,
And skipped through the hay feeling
very courageous.

He yelled to the children,

'Come, play with me!

'I'm Frank, I'm a UNiCORN,

fit as can be!'

Elsie's jaw dropped and she spluttered,
'Good grief!'
As the whole place stood still in
complete disbelief.

Frank kept on leaping and
bounding and prancing,
Till some of the children there
joined in the dancing.

Soon the whole place gathered round
the attraction,
Wanting a piece of the UNICORN action.

The animals loved it – they all
joined in next,
While the zookeepers stood there, aghast
and perplexed.

Bryan the hamster yelled,
'Check me out, girls!'
As he climbed on Frank's back and
held on to his curls!

'Yee-ha! Giddy-up!' yelled the hamster
with glee.
'Frank, you're not frightened –
it's so good to see!'

It went on for hours – the laughing
and petting
(But this time, none of this stuff
was upsetting).

GiDDY-UP!

Frank was now something else

deep down inside.

Not a silly alpaca . . .

This filled him with pride!

Then . . . amid all the merriment,

Frank heard a yelp

And a voice that screamed,

'Quickly – somebody help!'

YELP!

Frank swiftly turned,

very keen to find out

Just what the commotion

and fuss was about.

There in the fairground,

a child gave a squeal,

From a seat that was perched

high atop the big wheel.

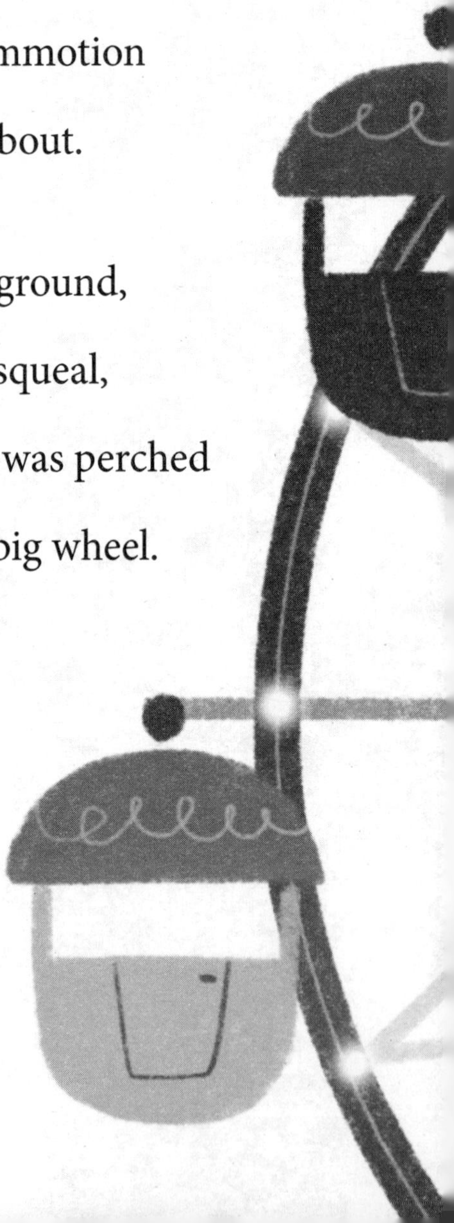

AAAAAHHHHHHH

It was Kim – Tim's big sister –

with such rotten luck.

She had ridden the wheel,

but the wheel had got stuck.

Now Kim was the one in

such dire circumstances . . .

(I can tell what you're thinking . . .

WOW, what are the chances?!)

'It's stopped!' poor Kim screamed.

'And I'm scared of heights too.

Help me!' she cried.

'I don't know what to do!'

How tragic! It seemed the old wheel
had packed in.
Its cogs were all jammed and would
no longer spin.

And Kim was high up on
that ride all alone,
With no others on it – just her on her own.

‘Call the fire brigade!’ yelled a man nearby.
‘It’s a job for the army!’ claimed one
random guy.

‘Get the cops!’ squealed Kim’s mother.
  ‘It’s a SWAT team we need,
They can swing from the framework
  and fix things with speed!’

Frank felt a shiver run
  right down his spine
As he knew in his mind . . .
  This was his time to shine!

‘I’ll save her!’ yelled Frank,
  his chest puffed with pride.
‘Give me some room.
  And now please – step aside!’

‘Wow!’ sighed the crowd with a
pleasing reaction,
As brave Frank stepped forward
and sprang into action.

CROSS
DO NOT CROSS

Like an oversized cricket, Frank leaped
with a bounce,
Over the barrier, not caring an ounce.

He climbed the wheel's metal
construction with ease,
And soon he was towering over the trees.

Frank knew he could do it.
No chance would he fall.
Frank was a UNICORN now, after all!

Coiled with Olympic-style
gymnastic flair,
Frank hurtled himself like a
bird through the air.

He did a back somersault,
just cos he could,
Thinking throughout to himself,
I look good!

Landing on top with such elegant grace,
Frank greeted Kim with a smile
on his face.

'I'm Frank, I'm a UNICORN,
hop aboard, please.
I'll have you back down
in a moment with ease.'

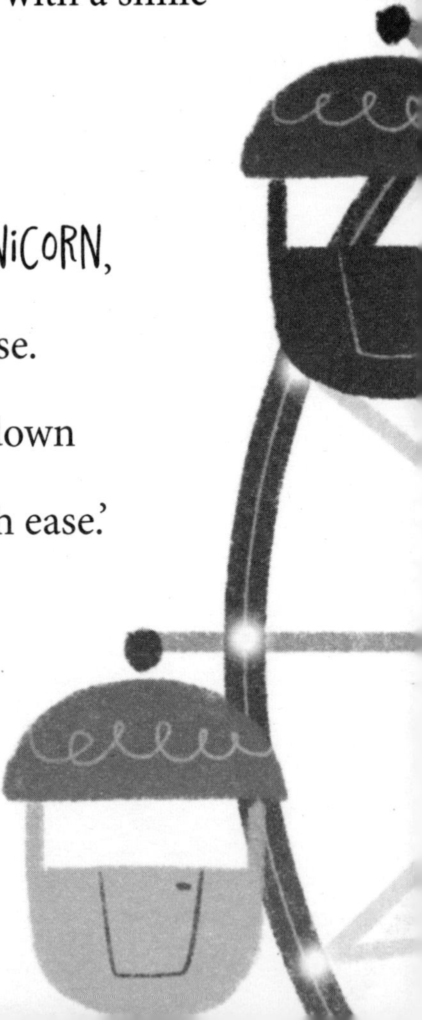

Confused, Kim just stared at him,

scratching her head.

She shrugged before answering . . .

'OK,' she said.

In no time at all, Frank had descended.

At last, this little girl's nightmare

had ended!

The crowd all went wild with complete

admiration

And yelled, 'Frank, we love you!'

in true adoration.

Kim's mother rushed over, hugged Frank
and she smiled,
Before giving a loving embrace
to her child.

She turned back to Frank and
leaned down to his ear.
'Well done!' she whispered and,
'Thank you, my dear . . .

'You're clearly a fearless alpaca
who's caring,
As well as being dashingly handsome
and daring!'

‘An alpaca . . . ?’ frowned Frank.

‘Oh goodness, not me . . .

‘I’m clearly a UNICORN now, can’t you see?’

The mum looked confused
(like her daughter had been),
So took a quick photo and
showed Frank the screen.

Poor Frank just
yelped when
he studied
the pic.

'My horn's disappeared!
My gosh – I feel sick!'

He was right, it had gone –
  just melted away,
As he played with the customers
  earlier that day.

But Frank hadn't noticed,
  he'd had too much fun,
Messing about in the afternoon sun.

Lost in his thoughts, Frank
  dropped to the ground.
Concerned, the people there
  all gathered round.

At first, Frank was broken

and grief-stricken too.

Until reality struck,

like a bolt from the blue!

All that confident playing,
the jovial dancing;
The children, the petting,
the bounding, the prancing.

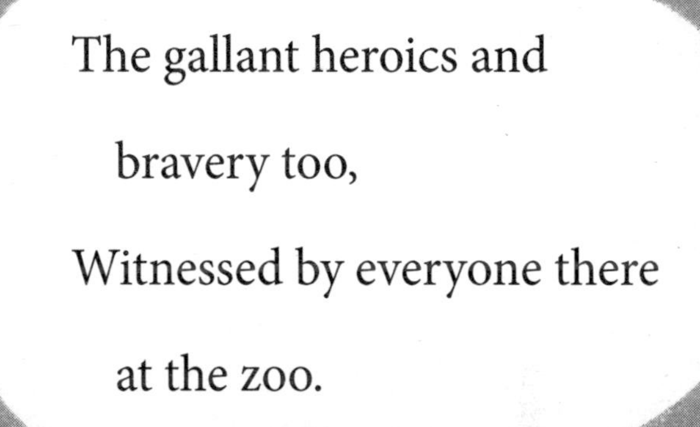

The gallant heroics and
bravery too,
Witnessed by everyone there
at the zoo.

It was him all along – no one
else there to thank.
That magical creature had
always been Frank!

So, with a deep breath, Frank rose
to his feet.
Now he felt certain his life was complete.

'Thank you!' he said – rather jovially.
'I *am* an alpaca. And I'm happy to be!'

And so, dear reader, we reach the
conclusion,
*But just so there isn't some doubt
or confusion . . .*

Frank's still at the zoo, in the
  petting enclosure,
Where now he gets masses
  of love and exposure.

He's happy at work and he's
  no longer stressed,
And the people who meet him
  all think he's the best.

The zookeepers even stock horns
at the zoo,
So the visitors there can be UNICORNS
too!

Even Bryan the hamster joins in
with the fun –
He has a horn too, just a
much smaller one.

Frank often wears one whenever he can
(He still has the book, and he's still
  a big fan!)

But now he feels different and
  happy within,
Tremendously comfortable
  in his own skin.

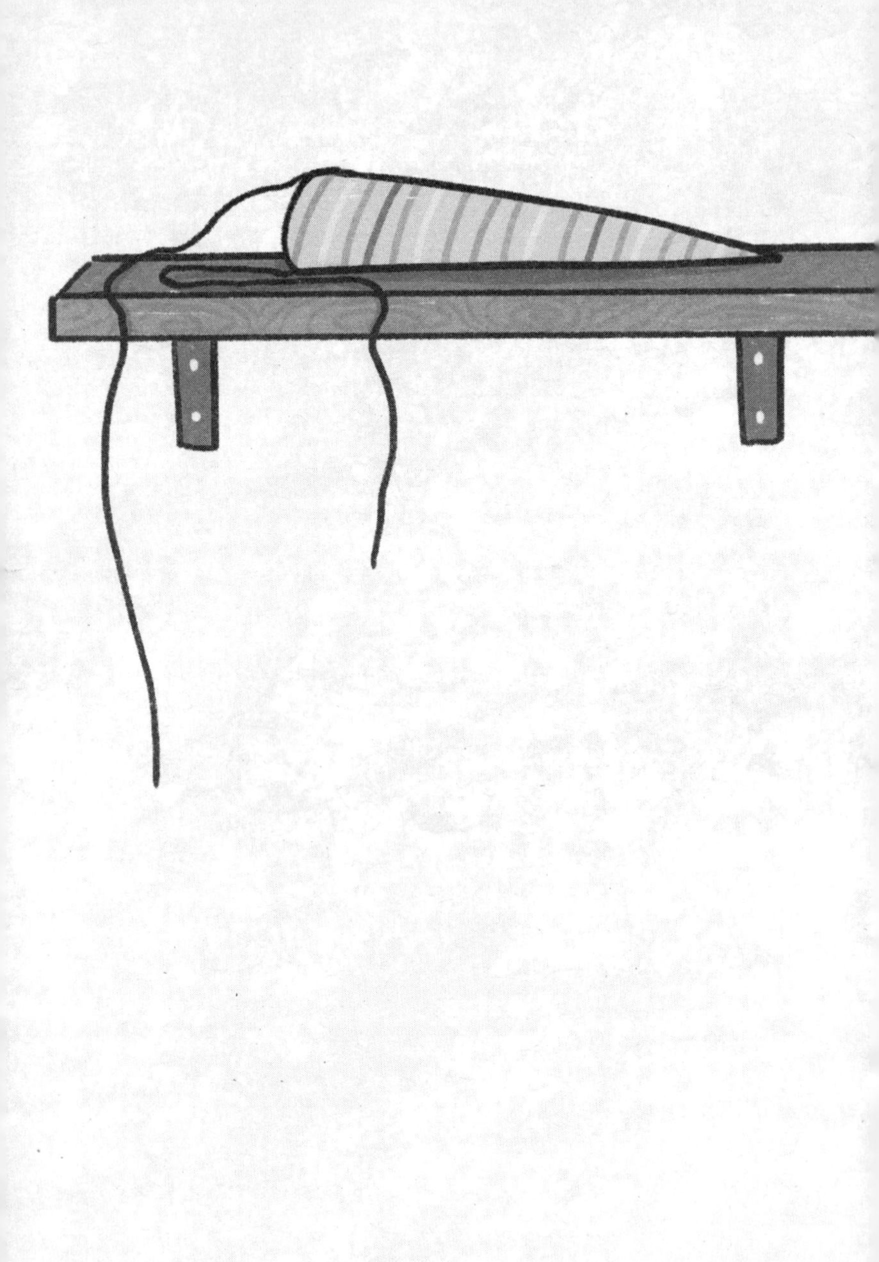

Sometimes he leaves his horn

on the shelf,

To have fun with the children . . .

and just be himself.

If you liked FRANK, you'll love the hilarious **Fables from the Stables** series: